Miss Malarkey Won't Be in Today

Miss Malarkey
Won't Be in Today

Judy Finchler
Illustrations by Kevin O'Malley

Walker & Company ✳ New York

First published in the United States of America in 1998 by
Walker Publishing Company, Inc.; first paperback edition published
in 2000.

Published simultaneously in Canada by Fitzhenry and Whiteside,
Markham, Ontario L3R 4T8

Library of Congress Cataloging-in-Publication Data
Finchler, Judy.
Miss Malarkey won't be in today/Judy Finchler; illustrations by Kevin
O'Malley.
p.   cm.
Summary: A teacher imagines the chaos that takes place when she
stays home one day because she is sick.
ISBN 0-8027-8652-9 (hardcover) −0-8027-8653-7 (reinforced)
[1. Teachers–Fiction. 2. Sick–Fiction. 3. Schools–Fiction.]
I. O'Malley, Kevin, 1961– ill. II. Title.
PZ7.F495666M1 1998
[E]–dc21   97-48729
ISBN 0-8027-7591-8 (paperback)   CIP
                                             AC

Book design by Sophie Ye Chin

Printed in Hong Kong
10 9 8 7 6 5 4 3 2

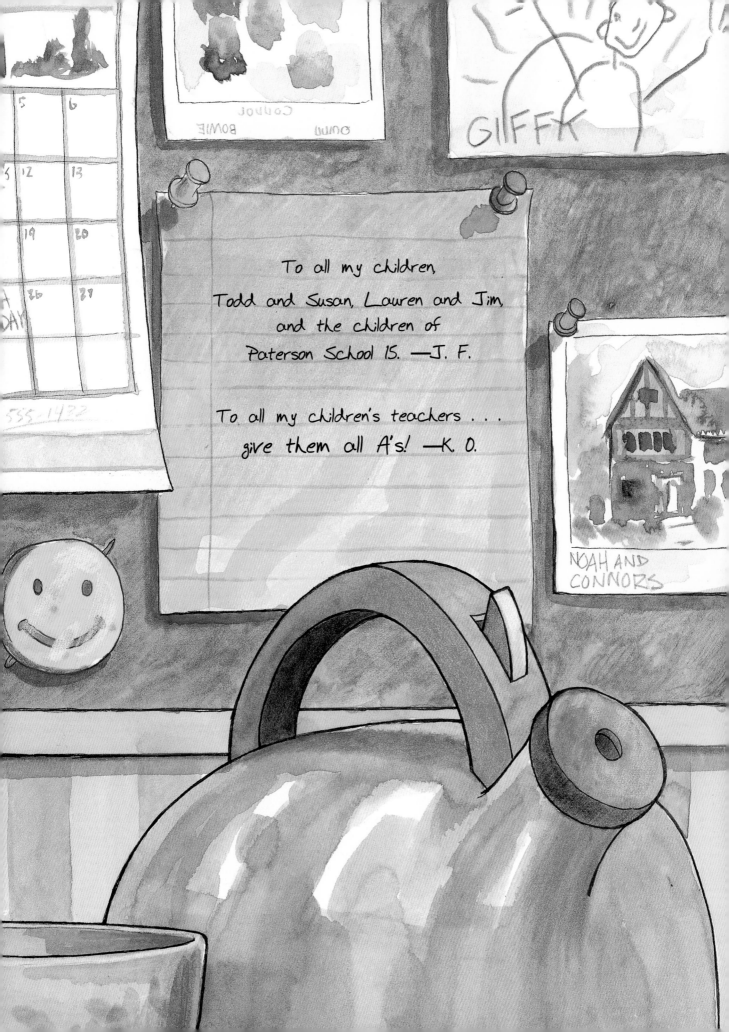

To all my children,
Todd and Susan, Lauren and Jim,
and the children of
Paterson School 15. —J. F.

To all my children's teachers . . .
give them all A's! —K. O.

I couldn't go to school this morning,
not with a fever of **103.2.**

I had to call Principal Wiggins.

Principal Wiggins doesn't *like* it
when a teacher calls in sick.

Then he has to find a substitute.

He hates finding substitutes.

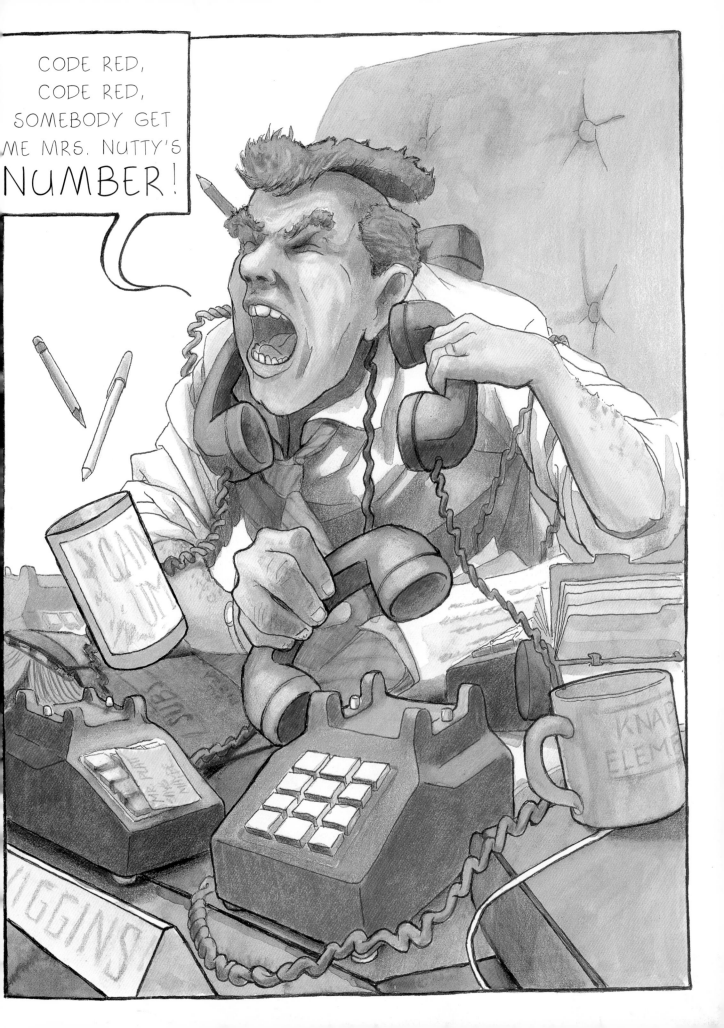

Oh,

and the last substitute he found

for Mrs. Boba's class didn't exactly work out.

My poor class!

What if he called Mr. Doberman?

That guy is so tough he even scares me.

Or he might have called Mrs. Ungerware.

The kids call her Mrs. *Underwear*.

Once my kids start laughing, they'll never stop.

Mrs. *Underwear* won't be able

to get anything done.

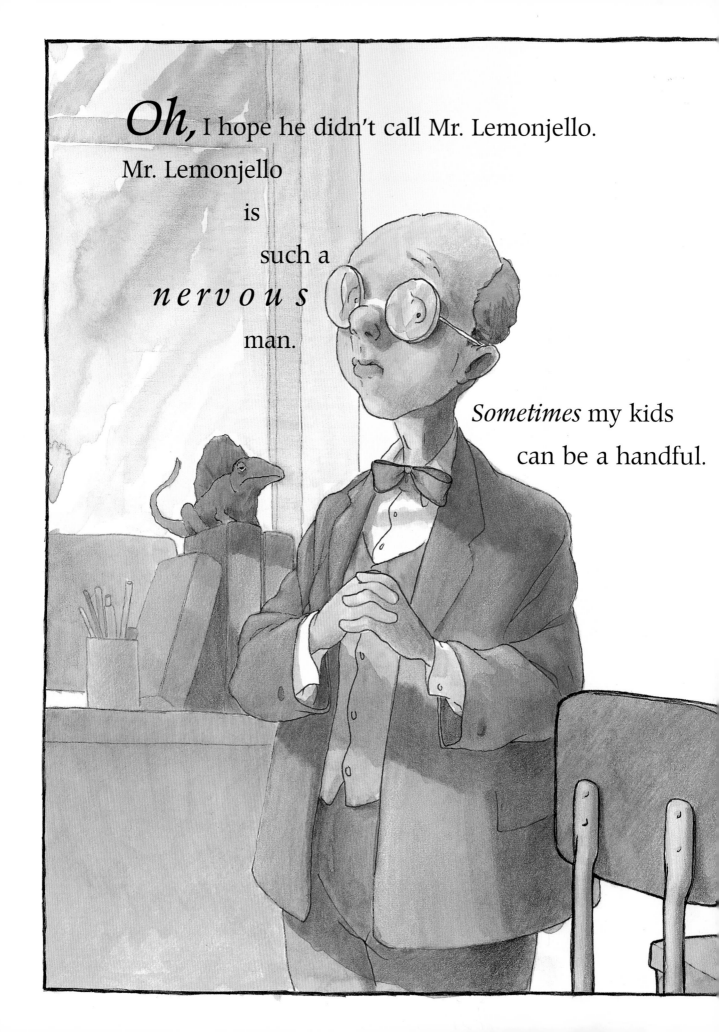

Oh, I hope he didn't call Mr. Lemonjello.
Mr. Lemonjello
is
such a
n e r v o u s
man.

Sometimes my kids
can be a handful.

He'll be scared **stiff** if they let
the iguana
out of its
cage.

He'll never be able to
handle them in music clas
They'll crank up the
volume.

They'll dance on the desks.
They'll swing from the lights.

And when they have art . . .

Oh,

when they have art, they'll go crazy.

They'll paint the ceilings and the floor.

Mr. Lemonjello will be two shades of

blue.

And then they'll all ask to go to the bathroom at the same time.

At the same time!

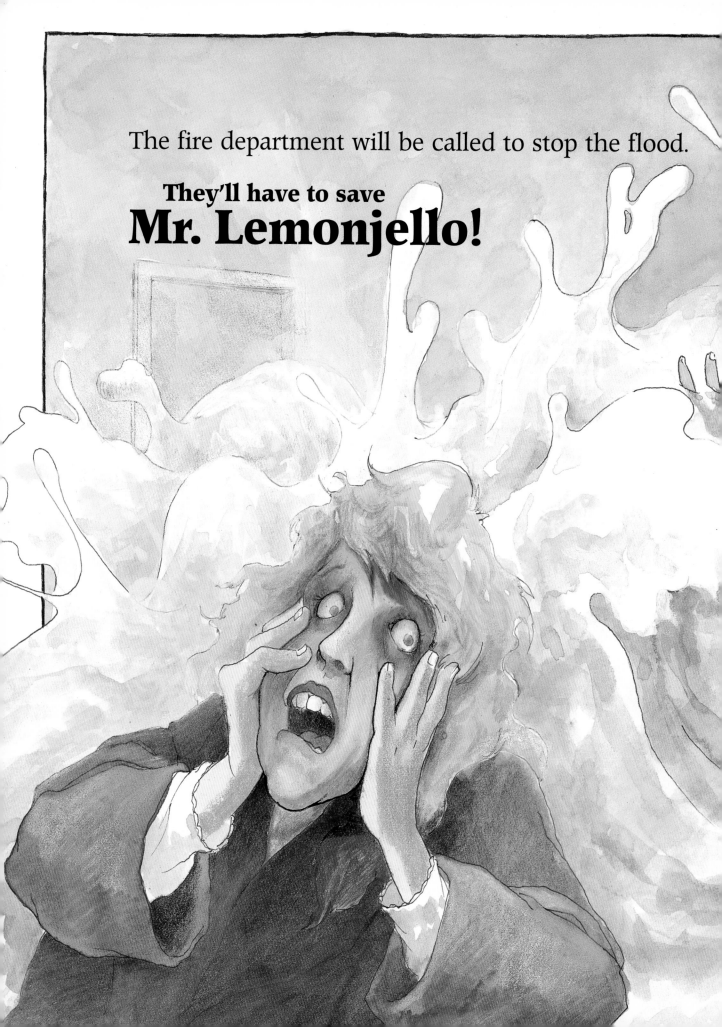

The fire department will be called to stop the flood.

They'll have to save
Mr. Lemonjello!

I have to get to school.

Right now!

Everyone looks okay.

Better than I imagined.

Better behaved than they are for me?

Oh, my class!

Oh, the bell!

Oh, my head!

"Miss Malarkey, where were you today?"
"Did Mr. Wiggins make you sit out here?"

"Oh, no. I didn't feel very well today,
    but I've been worried sick about everybody."

"We're fine, but you look terrible."
"Feel her head. Maybe she needs an ice pack."
"Let's take her to the nurse in case
    she needs to throw up."

"*Don't worry*, Miss Malarkey.
You just stay home and rest up."

"And if Mrs. Berpur is
our teacher tomorrow,
we'll take care of everything."

Oh no, not Ima Berpur!